Follow the winding stream to the
edge of the jungly forest and meet...

ZIGBY THE ZEBRA
OF MUDWATER CREEK.

Zigby the Zebra loves being outdoors, getting up
to mischief with his good friends, Bertie and McMeer.
There are always exciting new places to explore
and wonderful adventures waiting to happen
but sometimes he can't help trotting
straight into trouble!

Meet his friend, the African guinea fowl, **Bertie Bird**.
He's easily scared and thinks his friends are far too
naughty...but he'd hate to miss the fun, even if it does
mean getting dirty feathers!

McMeer is the cheeky little meerkat who
loves showing off and playing tricks. His practical
jokes sometimes cause all sorts of problems,
but he always knows how to have fun!

It was early morning in Mudwater Creek.
Zigby the Zebra was planning a day out in his canoe
with his friends, Bertie Bird and McMeer.
"Jump in, Bertie," said Zigby.

ZIGBY ™

HUNTS FOR TREASURE

BRIAN PATERSON

Collins

An imprint of HarperCollinsPublishers

Have you read all the books about Zigby?

Zigby Camps Out
Zigby Hunts for Treasure
Zigby and the Ant Invaders
Zigby Dives In

For William, Charles and Henry

First published in hardback in Great Britain by HarperCollins Publishers Ltd in 2002
First published in paperback by Collins Picture Books in 2003

1 3 5 7 9 10 8 6 4 2

ISBN: 0-00-713181-X

Collins Picture Books is an imprint of the Children's Division,
part of HarperCollins Publishers Ltd.

Text copyright © Alan MacDonald, Brian and Cynthia Paterson and HarperCollins Publishers Ltd 2002
Illustrations copyright © Brian Paterson 2002

Text by Alan MacDonald

ZIGBY™ and the Zigby character logo are trademarks of HarperCollins Publishers Ltd.

The authors and illustrator assert the moral right to be identified as the authors and illustrator of the work.
A CIP catalogue record for this title is available from the British Library.

The HarperCollins website address is: www.fireandwater.com

Printed and bound in Belgium by Proost

"Are you sure it won't tip me out?" Bertie worried.
"Hurry up!" urged McMeer. "I can't hold this picnic
basket for ever!"

Finally the three friends set off. They hadn't gone far when Zigby spotted something in the water. "Look! What's this?" he said, fishing out a bottle. He shook it and out fell a piece of paper. "It's a map!" exclaimed McMeer. "Give it to me, I can read maps."

The map showed a place called Parrot Island.
On it was drawn a rope bridge, a big cave, a snake
and a tree marked with an 'X'.
"I bet the 'X' shows where there's treasure!" said Zigby.
McMeer jumped up, shouting, "A treasure hunt!
Let's go on a treasure hunt!"

Soon they'd paddled far from home –
further than they'd ever been before.
"Down there!" McMeer pointed, checking the map.
Bertie felt frightened. He was sure they were
being watched. "Shouldn't we turn back now?"
he asked in a small voice.

"Are we nearly there?" asked Zigby.
"Stupid map!" grumbled McMeer. "It keeps folding
the wrong way."
"Sit down!" cried Bertie. "You're rocking the boat!"

Suddenly a gust of wind blew the map
right out of McMeer's hands…
…and into Zigby's face.
"I can't see!" he said in a muffled voice.
"Watch out, Zigby!" warned Bertie.

Too late – the canoe struck
a big rock and Bertie
toppled overboard.

"Help! I can't swim!" gasped Bertie.
"Grab this!" called McMeer, throwing the picnic basket
into the water. It sank slowly, along with all their food.

There was only one thing for it...

...Zigby jumped in to rescue his friend.

"It's okay, Bertie," laughed Zigby. "I can stand up here."
The rock they'd hit was close to a sandy beach.
As McMeer rescued the empty basket and pulled the
canoe on to the beach, a great flapping noise made the
three friends jump.
"Parrots!" said Zigby. "We've found Parrot Island."
"I *told* you I can read maps!" shouted McMeer.
"Let's go and find the treasure. Follow me!"

They followed McMeer up a steep path.
At the top was a long rope bridge.
"Here it is!" called McMeer.
"Hurry up, you two!"

"Stop making it wobble, McMeer," squawked Bertie.
"I'm going to fall."
"Don't look down!" warned Zigby.
They reached the other side safely but McMeer
ran on ahead.

"Look!" he said.
"I've found the cave."
"Do we really have to
go in there?" asked Bertie.
"There might be snakes!"
"Stay close to me,"
said Zigby, bravely.

They peered into the dark
cave and carefully they
inched forward.
Suddenly...

"OOH!"

They slid down the snake-like tunnel

...ntil... BUMP! "Ow! My bottom really hurts," moaned McMeer.

"AAGH!"

"OUCH!"

They spilled out of the cave, on to a beach.
"Look," said Zigby, "isn't that our canoe?
We're right back where we started!"
"Ooops!" said McMeer. "Stupid map."

"You can't read maps, can you?" groaned Bertie,
and he seized the map in his beak.
"Let go!" cried McMeer.
There was a loud ripping sound.
"Now you've torn it," said McMeer.

Bertie started to cry. "I want to go hooome!"
"Look, you two!" said Zigby. "Where are all those
parrots going?"

The three friends ran towards a clearing and found...

...the most amazing sight.
"It must be the tree on the map,"
said Zigby, "and it's covered
in fruit."

"All my favourite fruit!" said McMeer, licking his lips.

They ate and ate until they
were full to bursting.
"Delicious!" sighed McMeer.
"Yummy," sighed Zigby.
"But where was the treasure?"
asked Bertie, puzzled.
"On the tree, of course!" said Zigby.
"The best kind of treasure
is the kind you can eat!"

Later, the friends paddled away with their
basket full of fruit.

"What an adventure!" said Zigby.

"Yes," yawned Bertie. "Can we go home now?"

"I wish we had a map to get us home," said McMeer.

"No more maps," groaned Bertie.

"Never mind," smiled Zigby. "I think
we'll find the way without one."

"Thanks, parrots!"